P9-DGJ-833

The Perfect Pony

Kimberly Brubaker Bradley
pictures by Shelagh McNicholas

Dial Books for Young Readers

DIAL BOOKS FOR YOUNG READERS
A division of Penguin Young Readers Group
Published by The Penguin Group

Penguin Group (USA) Inc., 375 Hudson Street, New York, NY 10014, U.S.A.
Penguin Group (Canada), 90 Eglinton Avenue East, Suite 700, Toronto, Ontario, Canada M4P 2Y3
(a division of Pearson Penguin Canada Inc.)
Penguin Books Ltd, 80 Strand, London WC2R 0RL, England.
Penguin Ireland, 25 St. Stephen's Green, Dublin 2, Ireland (a division of Penguin Books Ltd)
Penguin Books India Pvt Ltd, 11 Community Centre, Panchsheel Park, New Delhi - 110 017, India.
Penguin Group (NZ), Cnr Airborne and Rosedale Roads, Albany, Auckland, New Zealand
(a division of Pearson New Zealand Ltd).
Penguin Books (South Africa) (Pty) Ltd, 24 Sturdee Avenue, Rosebank, Johannesburg 2196, South Africa.
Penguin Books Ltd, Registered Offices: 80 Strand, London WC2R 0RL, England.

Designed by Nancy R. Leo-Kelly
Text set in Raleigh Medium
Manufactured in China on acid-free paper
1 3 5 7 9 10 8 6 4 2

Library of Congress Cataloging-in-Publication Data
Bradley, Kimberly Brubaker.
The perfect pony / Kimberly Brubaker Bradley ; pictures by Shelagh McNicholas.
p. cm.
Summary: While searching for a sleek, fast, and spirited pony to own, a young girl comes
to realize that the "perfect" pony is actually very different.
ISBN 978-0-8037-2851-6
[1. Ponies—Fiction.] I. McNicholas, Shelagh, ill. II. Title.
PZ7.B7247Pe 2007 [E]—dc22 2004024071

The artwork was created using watercolor and a 4B pencil on watercolor paper.

To Katie, my pony girl

—K.B.B.

In memory of my dear Uncle Jamsie . . . the "perfect" uncle

—S.M.

Mom says that *pony* was my first word. I was pointing at my big brother's pony at the time.

As soon as I was old enough, I started riding Matthew's pony—in a lesson once a week.

And every single day I helped feed Matthew's pony and Mom's horse, and I helped clean the stalls and fill the water buckets.

Every day I looked into the third stall of our barn, the empty stall, the stall that could be for my pony. "Hurry, pony," I would whisper.

One day Mom heard me. “It’s time, isn’t it, Katie?” she said. “Time for your own pony. On Saturday we’ll start to look for one.”

I was too happy to yell. I made a noise that sounded like a squeak.

“Be patient, sweetheart,” Mom said. “Finding the right pony takes a long time.”

I am patient. I have been patient for years.

At night I dreamed about the perfect pony. He would be sleek and shiny, the color of toffee apples. Or he might be white, with sooty eyes and a delicate nose. My pony would be fast and spirited and beautiful.

On Saturday we drove to another barn.
I couldn't wait to see my pony.

The barn was big and busy. There were ponies everywhere. I looked at each one and wondered, Are you mine?

Finally a man led a prancing chestnut pony into the ring. He was tall and sleek. He shook his head and snorted. He was almost the color of a toffee apple. "He's perfect," I said.

Then the wind blew leaves across the ground. The pony jumped sideways. He tore the lead rope from the man's grasp.

"Yikes," I said. "Too nervous."

Mom put her arm around me. "Too young," she said. "But don't worry. There are lots of ponies in the world."

On Sunday we looked at a speckled white pony, with sooty eyes and a wide swayed back. "Hmm," said Mom. "Let's see him trot."

The woman holding the pony ran with him to make him trot. The pony limped.

"Oh, no!" I said. "Too lame."

Mom wrinkled her face. "Too old," she said.

I got to ride the third pony, but I couldn't make him trot. He walked in circles backward instead.

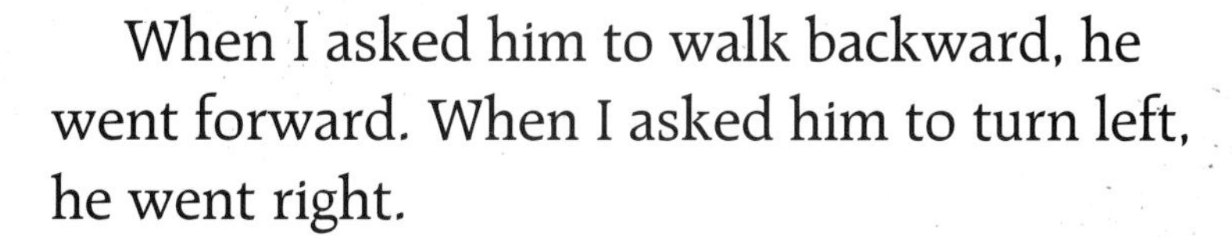

When I asked him to walk backward, he went forward. When I asked him to turn left, he went right.

"Too stubborn," I said.

"Too nasty," said Mom. "I'm sorry. Maybe we'll find one next weekend."

All week I drew pictures of perfect ponies. I drew black ponies and bay ponies, roan ponies and pinto ponies. They were tall and sleek and beautiful. Their manes looked like silver light.

The first pony we saw the next Saturday was a bay with a streak of white running down his face. His owner rode him around the ring.

He walked,

trotted,

and cantered.

He jumped a little pole. He looked as quiet as the lesson ponies at my riding instructor's barn. I felt full of hope.

Then I got on. The pony trotted when I wanted to walk. He cantered when I wanted to trot. When I steered him toward the pole, he put his head in the air and ran. I was so frightened, I closed my eyes.

Mom got the pony stopped and lifted me out of the saddle.

"Too scary," I said. "Too fast."

I wondered if I would ever find a pony.

Then, the very next day, we drove up to a small barn. In the pasture there were three horses and one little pony.

One round little pony.
One round, filthy little pony.

His owner brought him in. He was the color of mud, because he was *covered* in mud. His coat was as shaggy as a bear. His mane hung in clumps down to his shoulder. He shook himself, and dust flew everywhere.

"Too dirty," I said.
"Honey," Mom said, handing me a brush, "that can be fixed."

I groomed

and groomed

and groomed the pony.

After a while all the dirt was off of him. Most of it was on me. The pony liked it when I brushed him. He sighed and wriggled and touched his nose to my arm. I think he tried to smile.

He still looked round and shaggy. "He's not sleek," I said.
"That can be fixed too," said Mom. "Try him."

I rode him around the ring. He walked when I wanted to walk. He trotted when I wanted to trot. He stopped when I asked him to, and he cocked his ears back when I spoke to him. When I asked him to canter, he went along like a rocking horse. He seemed happy. I was happy too.

I rode back to Mom. She was smiling.

"He's perfect," I said.
And he was.